Dear Parent:

Buckle up! You are about to join your child on a very exciting journey. The destination? Independent reading!

Road to Reading will help you and your child get there. The program offers books at five levels, or Miles, that accompany children from their first attempts at reading to successfully reading on their own. Each Mile is paved with engaging stories and delightful artwork.

Getting Started
For children who know the alphabet and are eager to begin reading
• easy words • fun rhythms • big type • picture clues

Reading With Help
For children who recognize some words and sound out others with help
• short sentences • pattern stories • simple plotlines

Reading On Your Own
For children who are ready to read easy stories by themselves
• longer sentences • more complex plotlines • easy dialogue

First Chapter Books
For children who want to take the plunge into chapter books
• bite-size chapters • short paragraphs • full-color art

Chapter Books
For children who are comfortable reading independently
• longer chapters • occasional black-and-white illustrations

There's no need to hurry through the Miles. Road to Reading is designed without age or grade levels. Children can progress at their own speed, developing confidence and pride in their reading ability no matter what their age or grade.

So sit back and enjoy the ride—every Mile of the way!

For Carol
L.H.

For Debbie & Sophia
P.G.

Library of Congress Cataloging-in-Publication Data
Hayward, Linda.
Little by little / by Linda Hayward ; illustrated by Peter Grosshauser.
    p.   cm. — (Road to reading. Mile 1)
Summary: An adaptation of the Aesop fable, "The Crow and the Pitcher," in which a
clever crow figures out how to get a drink of water when another crow has given up.
ISBN 0-307-26117-4 (pbk.) — ISBN 0-307-46117-3 (GB)
[1. Fables. 2. Folklore.] I. Aesop. II. Grosshauser, Peter, ill. III. Title. IV. Series.
PZ8.2.H38 Li 2002
398.2—dc21
[E]

2001023237

A GOLDEN BOOK • New York
Golden Books Publishing Company, Inc. New York, New York 10106

ISBN: 0-307-26117-4 (pbk)
ISBN: 0-307-46117-3 (GB)

10 9 8 7 6 5 4 3 2 1

Little by Little

by Linda Hayward
illustrated by Peter Grosshauser

The sun is hot.
The creek is dry.

Two crows plop down,
too weak to fly.

Water! Water!
In a jar.

They try to drink,
but don't get far.

The top is narrow.
A beak is wide.

A big crow beak
won't fit inside.

One crow gives up.
He cannot drink.

One crow won't quit.
He tries to think.

He thinks until
he has a plan.

Crows can't go in,
but pebbles can!

Find a pebble.
Pick it up.

Drop it in the jar.
KERPLUP!

"The pebbles make
the water rise."

"It takes too long!"
the other cries.

One crow topples
in the sun.

One drops pebbles
one by one.

At last he knows
it's time to stop.

He sees the water
at the top!

When jobs seem big,
remember quick—

Little by little
does the trick!